THE ADVENTURES OF KELE:
BOY OF THE ROCK SHELTER

D1027545

RALPH E. JONES

ILLUSTRATED BY: JUAN HERNANDEZ AND DWAIN ESPER

AuthorHouse™
1663 Liberty Drive
Bloomington, IN 47403
www.authorhouse.com
Phone: 1-800-839-8640

Published by AuthorHouse 04/05/2012

ISBN: 978-1-4685-7696-2 (sc)

Library of Congress Control Number: 2012906003

Any people depicted in stock imagery provided by Thinkstock are models,
and such images are being used for illustrative purposes only.
Certain stock imagery © Thinkstock.

This book is printed on acid-free paper.

Because of the dynamic nature of the Internet, any web addresses or links contained in this book may have changed
since publication and may no longer be valid. The views expressed in this work are solely those of the author and do not
necessarily reflect the views of the publisher, and the publisher hereby disclaims any responsibility for them.

DEDICATION

This book is dedicated to my Grandchildren,

Drew, Rachael, Dean, and Lindsey;

and all of the young dreamers

who quest for adventure.

ACKNOWLEDGEMENTS

I thank my wife Chela for putting up with my frustration while writing this story.

The AuthorHouse editors and illustrators for their invaluable assistance in making this project a reality, and all of my dear friends and colleagues for their assistance.

Most notably, I am indebted to my Friend and Mentor, the saged Dr. Donald Smith, who aided me tremendously in reading, and pre-editing the draft; and just for being there for me. I also wish to thank my friends and mentors with the National Park Service, Mark Spiers and his daughters Lauren and Anna, and Rolando Garza; who have been very supportive; giving me the honored and special opportunity to practice vocational archaeology.

I am especially grateful to my dear friends Juan Hernandez and Stephen Vega for their unconditional support and counsel; with special thanks to Juan who was invaluable assistance in providing the initial illustration sketches and many others too numerous to mention here.

I am grateful to all of the Ranchers I had the privilege of knowing in West Texas, and for their welcoming me in exploring the many Rock Shelters from which the theme of this work is taken.

Finally, I owe a debt of gratitude to my many university professors who increased my love of the studies of archaeology; they planted the seeds which developed into this chapter of my life.

INTRODUCTION

Our story takes place about Eight Thousand years ago, in an area just east of the Big Bend National Park of West Texas. It was a very rugged, harsh, rocky, and mountainous place with many canyons and cliffs. Because the area was very dry with little rainfall, there was very little vegetation. The vegetation consisted of desert cactus, sparse small trees, and other plant life that had adapted over thousands of years to this arid and rugged environment. It was the land of the cave bear, the deer, rabbits, the panther, and other wild animals. It was a very difficult place for humans to live. It was on a cliff side, in a rock shelter above a very rugged canyon with a small river flowing through it that a boy named Kele was born. The rock shelter had a large opening high above the canyon floor, and was large enough inside for Kele and his family of twenty ancient cliff dwellers to live protected and in peace. Kele and his family were deep tan in color, had brown eyes, and long black hair. They wore leather bands around their head to hold their hair back, animal skins to cover their private parts. They wore sandals made out of plant material to protect themselves from the rocks, and wrapped their legs from the knee down with rabbit skins to protect them from the thorny plants. No one knows what language they spoke, but they possibly spoke a language that later evolved into the Puebloan-Aztec family of languages. The main characters in our story are Kele (Key-Lee), his father Kwahu (Qua-hu), his two uncles Katori and Akando, his two cousins Attu and Moki, and his mother Tawa. Kele was twelve years old and was coming into manhood, which meant that he would have to prove to himself and the family that he was ready to take on tasks of male adulthood. Soon he was to become a full member of his tribe by taking a hunting journey with his adult male relatives. If he proved to be brave and strong enough on this adventure then he would be welcomed into the tribe as a hunter and protector...an adult. This is his story.

CHAPTER 1

A New Day Begins

Kele awoke from his sleep with warm sunrays shining on his face, the sounds of people talking, and the sweet smell of something cooking. As he stirred on his sleeping mat, his thoughts turned to what he was to do this day, and he began to grow excited. His heart beat faster and he felt the adrenaline flowing through his muscles. Today was the day that his Father was to take him on his adventure...the adventure that would take him to man-hood.

Twelve hunting seasons had passed since his birth, and soon he would be accepted among the elders as a member of the tribe as so many others of his family had done for many generations. The paintings on the shelter wall next to his sleeping mat, with images of hunting, animals, shamans (shay-mans, a holy man), circles and lines of yellow, red and white; all reminded him of the stories told by his family.

He arose and stumbled over to the fire-pit in the great cave shelter, and joined his Mother, sisters, brothers, and other members of his family already eating their breakfast.

Kele was very pleased, as this morning there was roasted rabbit meat along with the roasted wild onions, sotol (so-tole, a plant with large rough edge leaves, with a root that is actually like a very large onion) bulbs, and yucca (yuck-ka), flowers to eat. He thought, "Soon I will be bringing home meat to my family, and they will welcome me as a full member of my people." "I will also kill the great panther and the Bear to protect my family and I will paint the cave walls with my adventures like my family has done for many generations before my time."

His mind wandered, until he was brought out of his day-dream with the sound of his Mother Tawa's voice, "Kele! Kele!" She called, "You day-dreaming boy. Eat your breakfast now as you must get ready to join your father Kwahu, your uncles, and your cousins who will go with you on your journey to manhood."

Kele ate his breakfast. The rabbit was warm and juicy, and the sotol bulbs had been cooking all night in the fire-pit coals and were very soft and sweet. He listened to his mother and other members of his family talk of him and the bravery he would show during his trip with his father. They also talked of other family members daring feats when they came of age.

Kele's eldest cousin, Attu, who had seen eighteen hunting seasons, began to tease him, saying "be careful that you do not get eaten by the big Panther Cat, they really like scrawny little sparrows like you."

Everyone began to laugh, even Kele. He knew the teasing was all in fun, as he remembered the teasing of other relatives when they prepared for their manhood adventure.

After eating, Kele put on his new woven sandals that his mother had made for him for this very special day. She made them from the leaves of the agave (ah-gah-ve, the agave plant has very large rough edge leaves which are very thick and contain a lot of juice) and lechuguilla (lay-chu-ghi-ya, the lechuguilla plant has thin, rough edged leaves with sharp tips) plants. He then put on his warm rabbit fur leggings to protect his legs from the cactus and other thorny plants.

He walked to the entrance of the huge sheltered cave which was the only home he had ever known. The cold season was now over, and the warm season had begun. He was so thankful, as his family had warmth and food to take them through the cold season. He looked out at the warm, rising Sun, and gave thanks to the Great Spirit for bringing back the Sun again for his people. His Mother and Father had taught him at an early age to always give thanks to the Great Spirit…for the new day, for his food, for protection of his family, for the plants and the animals, and especially for his life.

As the Sun rose higher, he looked out into the canyon below his shelter. The Sun colored the cliffs of the canyon, rocks, and the river below in bright colors of orange, red, green, and blue. The only noise he heard was the faint voices of those inside the shelter, an occasional bird, and the soft sound of the river flowing in the canyon.

Kele saw his Father, Kwahu, on a ledge below. He was knapping (flint rock is broken into thin pieces, then formed into a spear head, knife, or other tool) flint to make the spear points they would need on their journey. "Father," Kele said, "Are we almost ready to make our journey?"

"Yes," Kwahu replied, "I have almost enough points, and shall attach them to the spear shafts. We will need all we can carry in our quivers as we will probably be gone for 3 Sun rises. You go get our atlatl's (atal-atal, an atalatl is a piece of wood that has been smoothed with a raised part on one end. The spear is laid on the atlatl so that the end is held by the raised part of the wood. Then, the atlatl is held by one hand and the spear can be flung at a faster speed and further distance) ready, and a small amount of food." "Your Uncles and cousins are preparing their things to go with us."

Kele rushed back into the shelter with excitement. He picked up two of the Ataatl's (throwing sticks). Then going over next to the fire pit he gathered some food; placing it into a woven basket with straps that his mother also made for the journey. Finally he rolled up his woven sleeping mat, a net for trapping rabbits and fish both made out of Lechuguilla leave cords and his small bow and drill wood for making fire; and placed them all in his basket. Throwing the basket straps over his shoulder, he picked up the quivers and the atlatl's and then joined his father at the shelter entrance.

Kele's Father stood so tall against the Sun shadowed shelter entrance. Kele thought to himself, "When I grow up I am going to be just like my Father; strong, fearless and a real good provider for my family."

The Family all gathered around them to wish them good hunting. The Shaman then offered a prayer to the Great Spirit to watch over them, provide them strength and safety, and that they be able to find enough food and shelter along the way, and that Kele would hunt the deer to bring back to the family.

After all the goodbye's, Kele, his father, two cousins and two uncles were on their way. Kele's Father, Kwahu, led the way; followed by Kele, his Cousin Attu and his Father Adando, and last was cousin Moki (Moki was now 16 years old), and his Father Katori. Kele's Uncle Adando was Kwahu's eldest brother, and his hair was beginning to turn white with age. Katori was his second eldest brother, and had a scar on his face as a result of a panther attacking him when he was younger.

They carefully climbed down the rocky and brushy slope of the canyon wall, and soon they were at the bottom, at the rivers edge. From their cupped hands they drank of the cool, refreshing water. The Sun was beginning to rise higher now, and the canyon was beginning to become warm. Kele knew that by the time the Sun was straight overhead that it would become hot.

As he listened to the sound of the running water over the rocks, Kele noticed the changing colors of the canyon as the Sun began to rise higher. Looking out into the water, Kele saw the great Carp fish. He said to his Father, "Shall we try to catch the great carp for our dinner tonight?"

Kwahu answered. "Not today, Kele. We must follow the river up to the Great People Rocks while the Sun is still low. There will be time then to find some food to eat. We will stop at mid-day to eat the food that you brought."

Kele then said to the fish, "I will catch you at another time brother Carp, as we must be going now."

Kele had never gone beyond the rivers edge before, and each new step would be a new experience for him. He had heard the stories of the Great People Rocks as told by the elders of his tribe as they sat around the fire pits. He was not sure who they were, he only knew that the stories were a little frightening, yet he was eager to see who they were.

He knelt down into the river and gathered up a few fresh water clams, and put them in his bag. He enjoyed fresh water clams. His mother had sent him to the rivers edge before, with his cousins, to gather clams for the family.

His Father scolded him, "Kele, do not dawdle, or be distracted. Keep up with us."

Kele knew that no one in his family ever went anywhere alone, so he hurried to catch up with the others.

As Kele and the others continued up the rivers edge his uncles and cousins were talking about the animals that they might encounter on the trip. They talked of past hunting trips they had made, and their bringing home lots of meat for the family; the bison, the deer, rabbit, and other animals. They also talked of the dangers that they might encounter, recalling past events that they had experienced; the bears, the panther, snakes that rattle, and bad weather.

Kele listened to every word they spoke, as he was excited about the adventures they had and he thought "soon I will have my own stories to tell."

The Sun was straight overhead now and the canyon was beginning to get warmer. Kele knew that if they stayed by the rivers edge on their way that it would be cooler. He had not ventured so far from home before, and everything around him seemed strange; the plants were now bigger, the rocks and the cliffs were beginning to look different than those around his shelter home. He said to his father, "we have been traveling for a long time now, and the Sun is high. Isn't it time for us to rest and eat?"

His Father answered, "Yes Kele. You are right, it is time for rest." He then signaled to the others to stop and rest.

They all gathered in the shade of a small honey mesquite (mess-keet) tree, and began taking food out of their bags. Kele took some roasted rabbit, two sotol bulbs, and the clams that he had picked out of the river earlier, from his bag. As was the custom, he presented all of the food to his father, who in turn shared with him. The rabbit meat and the sotol tasted as good as in the morning, and the raw clams were a special treat. His uncles and cousins also began to eat the food that they brought.

"Tonight we shall have hot food, as we will hunt game along the way this afternoon", Kele's uncle said.

After eating and resting in the shade of the mesquite tree, Kele and the others began their journey again. Suddenly, coming around a bend in the river, Kele's Father signaled everyone to stop. Up ahead, close to the river was a cave bear. He was eating wild canyon grapes growing among the limbs an overhanging mesquite tree. Kele, along with the others, crouched down very close to the ground and moved slowly toward some brush and boulders away from the waters edge. Kele had never seen a real bear before, only the paintings on the shelter walls, and he became a little scared. "What are we to do?" he quietly asked his father.

"We must be very still and quiet Kele," said his father. We are not hunting bear on this trip and besides we do not have enough people with us to hunt the bear. We will just wait here a while and see if he goes away. There is no wind right now, and he does not see us or smell, us."

As Kele and the others watched the bear, Kele noticed how black the bear was, and the sun shining off his coat made him seem warm and friendly. The bear continued to eat grapes in a sitting position, and Kele laughed to himself in seeing his funny way of sitting. Kele also noticed the long and sharp claws of the bear, and he became a little frightened. He had heard the stories the elders use to tell about how the bears attacked, and especially the use of their strength and sharp, long claws. Suddenly, the bear rose up, and with a stretch, he began to waddle away from the rivers edge and up the steep canyon side. Kele watched until the bear was almost out of sight from their sheltered position behind the bushes, he said quietly to his father, "Brother Bear did not seem dangerous like the stories I have heard."

His father replied, "No, he did not. But remember this Kele, although the bear and other animals may seem friendly some times, they may be very dangerous at others. That bear had eaten his full of grapes, and maybe something else earlier. He did not see us, smell us, or hear us; so he did not believe he was in danger himself, and all he wanted to do is probably to go somewhere and rest. But if we were to try to hunt him he would know that he would be in danger from us, and all of us would be in danger."

Kele thought about what his father had said, then acknowledged his understanding with a nod.

Kele and the others, seeing that everything appeared okay, continued their walk up the canyon. The color of the canyon was changing to include darker browns and yellows, white and black, and reddish colored cliffs and rocks. The river was flowing a little bit faster than further down the canyon from where they had come, and Kele noticed the rippling effects and the increased sound as the water moved over the large rocks. The sun was now lower, and began to caste shadows across the canyon. Then, as if in an instant, Kele saw up ahead large rocks appearing to grow out of the canyon.

His father said, "we are coming to the people rocks soon Kele, do not be afraid."

As they walked nearer to the large rocks, Kele's uncle said, "There is a pool of water up ahead where the river has slowed, and at times there are animals there coming down from above the cliffs to drink. Many times we have made this trip, and there have always been animals there. But, we have to be very quiet, so we do not scare them away." Kele and the others walked along the brush very quietly, and the others began to take up their atl-atl's and spears. Then, Kele saw the pool of water, and drinking from it a small antelope.

Attu said, "There is our supper for tonight Kele." After placing spears in their atlatl's, they raised them and threw the spears at the antelope. The Antelope went down; a spear had found its mark.

"That was my spear," said uncle Katori, "I shall get the prize part for supper." Saying that, he flung the antelope over his shoulders and joined the others in their hike up the river.

It wasn't long until they came to the great people rocks. Kele looked in wonder at the huge rocks that appeared to grow out of the ground, with shapes that looked almost like statues of people. Kele said to his father, "The rocks do look almost like giant people. Are they spirits or people turned to rocks?"

His father replied, "I do not know Kele. They were here long before me or any other member of our family, and ancestors, can remember."

Kele replied, "They do not scare me as I thought they would. They almost look like they are guarding us."

As they walked by the large rocks, Kele's father said, "Look at the cliff above us, do you see a shelter cave up there?"

Kele looked up the canyon cliff, and he saw the shelter high above.

His father continued, "That is where we will be spending the night, it was the home of our ancestors."

Kele looked at the shelter high above, and thought how nice it would be to finally get to rest after their long days trek.

Kele and the others began the very steep climb to the shelter. Sometimes it was so steep that he had to grab a hold of bushes and pull himself up, and occasionally Kwahu would reach back and take his hand to help him along. His father, uncles, and cousins had all made the climb before and they seemed to have no great problem, although at times stopping themselves to catch their breath and watch their footing.

About halfway up, Kele looked at the shelter. It appeared much bigger now as they came near. It had two entrances divided by a slab rock in between. The left side entrance seemed to be cluttered with rocks, while the right side was very open. Keles cousins, Attu and Moke, were the first to reach the shelter, then his uncles, father, and then Kele. At the entrance way they all sat down to rest as they looked at the river below. They watched as the Sun began to go down, and the shadowed canyon began to turn to dark.

Kele's uncles began gathering sticks from around the shelter entrance in order to build a fire for the evening. Kele knew that they must have fire during the evening, not only for cooking, but to scare away the wild animals. Upon gathering enough wood, Katori went about making fire for a torch. He gathered up some dried grass, and with his bow and drilling stick began to start the fire. Kele watched carefully as he knew that his turn would come to make fire.

Katori moved the bow and drilling stick very fast across a small piece of wood until the wood began to smoke. He then placed dry grass onto the wood, and soon the grass began to burn. The others took the wood into the shelter, toward the rear, and stacked them up with dried grass in between.

Katori, using the torch, set the wood and grass on fire. Kele looked around the shelter in amazement as the light from the fire danced around pictures on the walls. The pictures were not like he was used to seeing in his shelter. There were no animals or people. There were yellow circles, straight lines, long neck figures, squares and rectangles, wavy lines, and red filled in circles.

He asked his father, "What does all of this mean?"

His father replied, "These paintings were placed here many thousands of seasons ago by our ancestors, the ancient ones. We do not know what all of them mean, but we believe that it is the way they saw the world during their time. But if you look closely at this one you will recognize it as a shaman. Do you see the long neck and body?"

"Yes father," Kele replied. "But the others look so frightening and strange."

His father said, "At sun-up you will be able to see the pictures better, and maybe they won't be that frightening to you."

Before the sun set further, they all stepped out of the shelter to gather more wood for the fire as they would need enough to last through the night. Once back inside, Kele's uncles and cousins prepared the antelope for cooking. They also spread out their woven sleeping mats around the small fire, and laid their atlatl's, spears, and baskets on the mats.

As the meat was roasting over the fire, everyone talked of the day's events and the long hike up the river to the rock people and the ancient ones shelter. Kele really liked hearing the stories and added his thoughts to the conversations.

After eating, now tired and with full stomachs, all but Kwahu laid down on their mats to sleep. Kwahu was to take the first watch and to keep the fire going, for the shelter people must be alert all night for animals, and perhaps other people, who may want to attack them.

Kwahu turned to Kele and said, "Sleep well my son, for tomorrow we go above the canyons to the great plain to hunt game for our family, and you must prove yourself by taking part in the hunt."

Kele replied, "good night father, and I will make you proud tomorrow." After saying this, Kele drifted off to sleep.

CHAPTER 2

THE SECOND DAY:

The Day Of The Hunt

Kele had drifted off to sleep and started to dream. His dream began with his looking at the paintings on the shelter wall. The pictures came to life and began moving around. The circles were turning around and around, the lines began to cross each other, and the shaman painting began dancing. The fire in the shelter was smoking more and Kele saw figures dancing around the fire pit. Their faces were painted and they carried spear shafts. Around and around they went, and up and down; stomping the dust of the shelter with their feet and singing loudly. They motioned to him to dance with them, and he then knew that they were his ancestor spirits. As he danced and made noises with them he saw himself with paint on his body and feathers in his hair; holding his spear and atl-atl. He danced around and around, stomping his feet with the other spirits and feeling joy in his heart. Kele suddenly heard a voice calling his name, first very softly and seeming far off. Then the voice sounded louder, "Kele! Kele!" the voice called.

Kele awakened suddenly to the sound of his father's voice, the sound of thunder, shouting, and loud grunts and squealing. As he awakened completely, he saw the shadows of his father and the others in the shelter opening fighting off a band of javelinas (have-a-leenas), like wild pigs with very long and sharp tusks). They were trying to come into the shelter to seek cover from the rain, which was coming down very heavily.

Kele at first became very frightened with the lightning, thunder, and the sounds of his relatives and the animals; but became very alert when his father shouted, "Kele! We need you. Bring your spear over here and help us!" Kele at once jumped to his feet, and grabbing his spear joined the others in the fight. He hurried between Kwahu and Attu and began to poke his spear at a javelina, which was squealing and grunting loudly with his tusks shining brightly and foaming at the mouth. Kele stuck the pig in the nose and mouth with his spear causing the pig to jump backwards, then losing his footing he tumbled down the hill into the river below. Kele was unaware that he had knocked out the Boars tusk during the fight. Suddenly, a javelina in front of Kwahu rose up on his hind legs, and as he did Kwahu plunged his spear into the pig's chest. The javelina went over backwards and began to roll down the steep hill and also ended up in the river below. The other javelina's became frightened and started to run out the shelter toward a narrow path leading upward to the right, and disappeared into the darkness. Kele and the others looked at each other and then began to whoop and yell as the excitement of defeating the javelina's overcame them.

They were all wet from the rain and went back into shelter by the fire to get dry and warm.

Kwahu said to Kele, "my son, you showed a lack of fear and great courage in that fight, and I am very proud of you. Tonight you have shown us that you are to be a protector of our people, and on the right path to manhood."

Kele's uncles and cousin Attu all began to yell in agreement, chanting "Kele, Kele!"

Kwahu felt something below his sandal, and reaching down he picked up a tusk that had broken out of the Boars mouth that Kele had fought with. He quietly put it in a small deer skin bag he carried under his breach cloth strap.

The storm clouds and the rain began to move away, and Kele and the others began to dry off as they sat by the fire. They were all tired and sleepy and returned to their mats. Kele's uncle remained by the fire to keep it going through the rest of the night. Kele watched the dancing flames of the fire until his eyes became heavy; he felt comfort and peace in his heart. He then drifted back to sleep.

Kele awoke to the smell of meat cooking on the fire pit, and the sound of his father, uncles, and cousins moving about the shelter. The Sun was just rising, and the rays of light were dancing off the cliffs across the canyon. The storm had passed, and as Kele walked toward the shelter opening he smelled the fresh, clean odors of the brush and grass one smells after a rain.

Kwahu joined him at the entrance and giving him a gentle slap on the back asked, "Are you aching after the fight last night Kele?"

"No Father, I am a little sleepy that's all."

His father replied, "I am very proud of the way you fought the wild hogs with us last night, and you have proven that you can help your family when they are in danger. As you have taken the steps toward completing your journey to man-hood, it is time that you started to take on more responsibilities on this trip; to get up earlier, to help with the fire, to help with the cooking, and to take your turn keeping the fire going and guarding everyone at night. I believe you learned last night that there are dangers, and most especially at night, and we must all do our part as a family. Now we eat and continue our trek to the hunting grounds."

Kele looked at his father with great admiration. He had so much on his mind to say to his father, yet he could only manage to say "Thank you Father. I will proudly do my duties as your son and a member of the family, and I promise that I will do my best to do the right things." His Father smiled at him and nodded his satisfaction.

After eating and putting rocks over the fire, the small group collected their hunting equipment and left the shelter. They then began climbing the steep path that led to the land above the canyon. The going was rough, as the pathway became steeper and steeper. The path finally came to the base of the cliff.

Kele's Uncle said, "This is the shortest of the cliffs that lead up to the big land above. It will be hard for you to climb Kele, as this is your first time. Just walk where we walk, and hold onto the rocks that we use and you will do fine. Try not to look down toward the canyon just look where you are standing and where you put your hands." Kele followed his uncle, and the others trailed behind to keep their eyes on him. Kele made sure that his basket and spears were tight over his shoulders, and that his sandals were still in good shape. They then began to climb the face of the cliff.

Slowly and carefully the group began climbing to the top. Kele's uncle said, "Don't look back down Kele, watch where I put my hands and feet, and stay close."

The climb became more difficult, but Kele grabbed the same hand-holds on the cliff face, and placed his feet where his uncle did.

The climb was going well, and then, a snake that rattles came out of a crack in the cliff between Kele and his uncle. Kele yelled to his uncle, "Uncle! The snake that rattles is on the small ledge where I am to grab hold of, what am I to do?"

"Stay where you are Kele," his uncle said, "I will try to turn around and help you."

Kwahu called from behind Kele, "Kele, I am right below you."

Kele became afraid and looked down to see his father, and lost his footing. "Father! He said. "I am going to fall!"

25

Kwahu grabbed Kele's ankle, saying, "Do not worry Kele, I have you."

Meanwhile, Uncle had taken out one of his spears, and jabbing it at the snake he tossed it far to the side of Kele. "Every thing is okay now Kele, the rattlesnake is gone." Saying that he reached down and grabbed Kele's hand, pulling him back to the small ledge he was standing on.

Kele was very relieved, and thanked his uncle and father for saving him. All the others also gave a sigh of relief. They then continued their short climb to the top of the cliff.

As they reached the top of the cliff, they all sat down to rest. Kele looked down from edge of the cliff and saw the river as it snaked through the canyon. It seemed so small from up here, he thought, but seemed to go on forever. Turning around, he saw the great plain and hills before him. Far in the background, behind the hills, he noticed mountains. The plain was spotted with trees and some dense brush, and there were large boulders spotting the landscape. Living all of his life in the canyon, he had never seen such vast space before, and with mouth open he stared in awe.

His father interrupted his almost trance like state, saying to him, "This is where we will do our hunting Kele. It is where all of your family has hunted for as long as can be remembered. It is in this vastness that the deer, bison, antelope, wolves, mountain lions, javelina, and other animals roam. With the spirits guiding us, we will take home enough food for our family to last through the dry season."

As everyone was getting their things together to continue the trip, Kele's Father said, "There are some very important things that you need to know when we go across the open spaces, you will have to remember what I am now going to tell you. It is very important that we all stay together, and watch where everyone is at all times. You must keep quiet, and listen to everything we say. We do not want to scare off any animals that we are hunting, and we do not want anyone to be in danger. Do you understand Kele?"

Kele replied, "Yes Father, I understand and I will listen to you, uncles, and cousins and do everything all of you tell me to do."

Kwahu then stated, "Your Uncles and Cousins here have been on hunts before, and they will be depending on you to be active in the hunt. We will not be able to carry our animal carcasses and be home before dark, so we will go to a cave that we have used for many seasons to stay for the night, and then we will head for home as the Sun rises. Let us only hope that the animals are plentiful this day, and that the Great Spirit smiles on us and provides us a good hunt. Now, everyone check that your atlatl and spears are at the ready, that your sandals are secure, and your baskets are tightly bound to you." When everyone had checked their equipment, Kwahu then motioned to move forward onto the plain.

It was now mid-morning as the small group of hunters moved out onto the plain. Kele was fascinated by the large flat plain, as well as the hills and mountains in the background. There were large boulders and trees dotting the landscape, blending into the tall grass and occasional brush.

Following Kwahu, the group headed toward a small area of trees. Keles uncle Akando told Moki to climb up a tree and see if he could spot a herd of animals anywhere. Moki, then climbed up the tree, taking his time to avoid thorns, until he could not climb further. Everyone watched him as he looked all around from his perch on a high limb.

He then motioned that he was coming down, and when he reached the bottom he said quietly, "There is a herd of more than 25 deer toward the hills. And further across, on the open plain, there is a large herd of Bison."

Kwahu then stated, "We are not enough numbers to go for the Bison, so we will have to hunt the deer. With the six of us we can probably carry three deer back home, as they are much smaller than the Bison." Upon saying that, he motioned for everyone to move on again toward the deer herd.

The group, led by kwahu, moved from brush to brush to get closer to the herd of deer. Finally they were close enough to see the deer, and began to crouch down into the tall grass, moving more slowly and quietly toward the herd.

Kwahu then said, "Akando, you and Attu move around the left side of the herd; Katori and Moki will move around the right side; and Kele and I will move in from this side. Once you are in place, and get your atlatls and spear shafts ready, we will be able to charge into the herd. I will give you time to move around to your positions, and then we will charge the herd all together upon my signal. Remember you must be quick in selecting your deer and taking proper aim, as they will run away very fast."

Kele could feel his heart beating faster as he awaited his Father's order to charge the herd of deer. He had his atlatl with a spear shaft at the ready, and only hoped that he would be able to do what he was expected to do. He knew that they must have meat if the family were to make it through the dry summer. Suddenly the wind started to blow a little and the deer rose up their heads from grazing. They smelled the men and started a panic through the herd.

Kwahu stood up and said, "Now!" At the command everyone started to charge toward the herd. The deer began leaping and running, but were trapped on three sides and became confused. Attu was first to throw his spear and Kele saw a deer go down. Then Kwahu brought down another. Kele flung his spear at a deer just as it leaped into the air, and then noticed that the deer was hit with another spear. Looking around, he saw that his cousin Moki had tossed the spear, hitting the deer at the same time as Kele's.

Kwahu yelled, "Enough! We will only kill what we can carry and we have got our three." Besides, he continued, "You all know that we do not kill our brother deer except what is needed for our food. The Great Spirit would be angry if we killed more. Now, let us prepare these three deer to carry home."

There was much excitement in the group, but especially with Kele. This was his first hunt, and he wanted to dance with joy. He thought, "Now will I become accepted as an adult in the tribe? Surely I must be accepted as I helped fight off the javelina, and now helped to kill a deer."

Moki, said to Kele, "We hit the deer at the same time little sparrow, that was very good shooting."

Everyone else agreed with him, and his father said, "That was very good throwing Kele, all of your years of practicing with your atlatl have prepared you for this day. I am proud of what you have done so far on this trip yet we still have a ways to go before reaching our home."

With the deer over their shoulders, the group started on the trail back home. Kwahu said to the others, "We will be returning home on another trail. It will be an easier trail. We will cross a small creek where we will rest. Then we shall spend the night in a small cave before heading off to home. The trail will then take us to the far end of our canyon where it will be much easier to go down into with our load of deer."

The sun was nearing mid-afternoon now, and was becoming warm. Katori and Attu led the group as they followed single-file. The Uncles, who were taller and stronger than the rest, carried a deer over their shoulders. Kwahu carried the largest deer, a male, with antlers. Kele was so proud of his strong father, noticing how he carried the deer with ease.

Still tired from the hunt, Keles legs were becoming heavy as they continued their walk. He was becoming thirsty and hungry, but did not want to show weakness in front of the others. His father, sensing that everyone was becoming thirsty and hungry, said "In a short time we shall come to a small stream, and there we shall rest a while and catch rabbits for our dinner. We cannot cook them though, as the smoke and cooking meat will attract the great cat and wolves. We will eat yucca flowers and others plants for now, and then we shall enjoy our dinner in the safety of a rock shelter not very far from the stream." Katori and Akando agreed with Kwahu, as they had made this same trip many times before also, and knew that Kwahu was right.

After what seemed like hours to Kele, the group heard the sound of running water. Soon they could see the stream as they came upon an arroyo. The stream had small trees and bushes along its banks, and the water was crystal clear. The group walked down into the arroyo toward the creek. At the creeks edge they laid down the deer, their baskets, atl-atl's and stooped down to drink of the cool, clear water. They all took off their sandals and sat down by the creeks edge with their feet in the water. After that long walk, Kele thought, the water feels so good on my burning feet. Soon, everyone was sighing with relief, and began to splash each other with the water.

Katori, an older, more serious brother, said "It is good to splash in the water, but don't you all know that we must find food to eat now, and then catch some rabbits before it starts getting late?"

They all agreed with Katori . Putting their sandals back on they began to search the bushes and trees for something to eat. Picking wild persimmons, wild onions, and canyon grapes; they piled everything up on a flat rock and sat down to eat.

Kele bit into a ripe persimmon, and the juice started running down his chin. "I am very hungry, and this persimmon is so sweet and juicy, but I wish we had some hot meat or fish to eat" he said.

Everyone nodded their head in agreement, but they also knew that they would have to wait until they came to the shelter in the rocks before they could have a hot meal. Kele noticed Kwahu picking up small rocks from the bottom of the creek and along the bank. "How curious," he thought. "Father has been picking up rocks since we were in the shelter. I wonder what they are for?"

Kwahu rose from his squatting position and said, "talking of meat, we must now hunt some rabbits on the way for dinner tonight." They all stood and gathered their equipment, and Kwahu and the uncles, after giving their atlatl's to moki and Kele, picked up the deer and again put them over their shoulders. They started up the arroyo embankment and followed a well worn trail across the plain again. "Usually we see rabbits along this trail," said Kwahu. He then motioned to Attu and Kele and said "get out your nets and see if you can catch some." Then handing the atlatls to Moki, they began walking toward the side of the trail.

Kele and Attu took their nets from their baskets, and began a search for rabbits in the brushy areas besides the trail, insuring they did not lag too far behind the group. Kele studied each patch of brush, kicking rocks as he walked hoping to scare a rabbit out of its hiding place. With the net that his mother had woven for him in hand, he noticed movement in a bush. As he neared the bush, a rabbit hopped out and started to run away. With a flick of his wrist, Kele threw his net, trapping the rabbit. He then said to Attu, "Look Attu, I have caught the first rabbit."

No sooner than he said that when Attu also flung his net at a startled rabbit, also trapping it. Within a few more minutes, they captured 3 more rabbits. Grabbing the rabbits by the ears, they then rejoined the group. All were laughing and talking about the rabbits and the "great hunters" who had netted them. Kele was certainly happy, and thought about having roasted rabbit for dinner.

His Father said, "first you attacked the javelina, then you brought down a deer, and now you have trapped rabbits. This has been a very good first hunt for you and I am very proud that you are my son."

The Sun was now very low in the sky as they continued on the trail. Everyone became somewhat tense, as they knew they must be in a shelter before sunset or else animals would attempt to take their deer and rabbits from them. Suddenly, Kele noticed large boulders and rocks ahead of them.

Katori said, "At last we have reached the cave shelter. I am really looking forward to a good dinner, rest and sleep," as he shrugged his shoulders and readjusted the deer he was carrying.

Adando agreed saying, "this deer is getting to be very heavy, but it is just a few more steps and we will rest."

The others agreed, saying how tired and hungry they were.

Just when Kele thought that he could not take another step, he saw the small cave among the boulders. "We have walked so far and done so much this day Father," he said, "I just want to lie down and rest."

His father replied, "Yes Kele, we are all very tired and hungry. This has been a long day. But look what the Great Spirit has provided for us this day. Isn't it really worth it to know that the family will be most pleased with the deer we bring back and the story you will have to tell them about your adventure?"

Kele said, "Yes father, I am excited to tell them and to know that I helped with the hunt."

Katori, his uncle, said, "Do not get too excited yet little sparrow, the trip is not over yet. We still have to stay in the cave for tonight and guard our deer. Then tomorrow we have to go down into the canyon and up the river to our family shelter. We will have to be ready for anything."

Kele, thinking about the Bear, when the javalina's attacked them, the rattlesnake on the cliff, and the danger running among the deer; certainly agreed, and his excitement was gone. All he could think about was having the courage and strength to go on.

As they came to the opening of the cave, Kwahu entered to see if there were any animals inside. He came out and motioned for everyone to go inside. The cave was very dim and cool, and also had an unusual smell about it since man and animals had been using it for a long time. It was just large enough for the group and the deer and not much bigger.

Keles uncles placed the deer at the back of the cave, and then returned to the opening. Kwahu instructed Attu and Moki to find wood for a fire, but not to walk to far from the cave. Then he and the uncles went about preparing the rabbits for dinner.

Attu and Moki returned to the cave with their arms full of wood for a fire. Kele gathered some dry grass, and reaching into his basket he took out the fire making kit. Moving his bow with the drill back and forth, he eventually produced enough heat by friction to set the grass afire. He added wood to the fire, and soon there was enough fire to light the cave entrance, and to cook rabbit for dinner. His father and uncles had completed preparing the rabbits for dinner and placed them over the flames. Everyone sat around the fire, eagerly awaiting the rabbit to be roasted.

The Sun was now setting, and Kwahu said, "We must gather up enough wood to last through the night." He arose and went outside the cave for more branches for the fire. Kele, Attu, and Moki immediately followed him. Katori and Akando remained by the fire tending to the cooking.

It was now getting dark and somewhat difficult to see. Kele had not experienced going outside of shelters at night and he was a little frightened. He gazed at the heavens in astonishment, looking at the vast amount of stars in the sky. He had seen stars before quite often when looking out of the shelter home, but never so many at one time as now. He always wondered what the lights in the sky were, but no one would ever give him an answer when he asked about it, other than: "they are lights given to us by the Great Spirit."

Suddenly, his concentration was broken by his Father saying, "Kele, stop your day dreaming and collect wood. It is getting dark and we must go back into the cave." Kele quickly gathered up all of the wood he could find and headed back into the cave with the others.

Katori and Akando were already eating the rabbit when the others came back into the cave. Everyone else dropped their wood by the wall of the cave and sat down by the fire. They all grabbed a piece of the roasted rabbit and wild onions and began to eat rapidly, as they had very little to eat the entire day.

Katori appeared somewhat nervous, and said "We must be very alert tonight as we have 3 deer and some rabbits in the cave. The panthers and the wolves would like very much to visit with us tonight to see if they can rob our catch."

Kwahu replied, "Yes, I am afraid you are right. We must increase our watch to 3 of us with atlatl and spears at the ready. I have already seen the shadow of the great panther not far in the distance. Katori, Moki, and Attu will take the first watch, and you will awake I and the others in a little while. We must not let the animals get to our deer and rabbits. Before we go to sleep, I made something for Kele along the trail." Then, turning to Kele, he reached into his pouch and pulled out a necklace made from bright, shiny stones with a javelina's tusk in the center.

Kele stood in awe while inspecting all the stones and the tusk. He explained with glee," Father it is beautiful, and I thank you so much. I saw you picking up stones along the trail, but I did not know why you were doing it."

Kwahu answered, "You have proven yourself to be a warrior and great hunter, and you deserve this totem. And you will be known at our shelter celebrations as 'Kele: the Javelina Slayer.'

Everyone laughed and whooped with Kele as they were so proud of him. "The journey is not quite over yet," said Kwahu, "and we will wait until we get home to have the real celebration of your man-hood. In the mean time we still may face great perils and dangers on the last part of our journey." Saying that, he motioned to everyone to go to sleep or do guard for the evening.

Kele was awakened by his father from a nice dream, seemingly a short time after going to bed. "It is time you take Moki's place at guard Kele, and make sure you keep the fire going well as there are wolves and panthers about." Kele arose, and took his atlatl and spear sheaf toward the shelter opening. The others had been relieved, and he joined his Father and uncle Akando by the fire.

CHAPTER 3

THE THIRD DAY:

The Journey Home

Kele awoke again from a pleasant dream with the smell of rabbit and sotol's roasting, and the sound of his relatives talking around the fire pit. Attu, was also rising from his sleep and explained, "Morning all ready? I am still so sleepy."

Katori, said, "Get up and have something to eat my son, we must be off on the last part of our journey, and you will need your strength."

Attu replied to his father, "Yes father, but I would rather be sleeping more."

Kele felt the same way as he began eating his meal.

His guard time was rather quiet last night, with exception of a few wolves howling and the panthers roaring in the distance. He knew that he only had a few hours of sleep, but was eager to continue the journey toward home. He thought to himself how tired he was and how he missed his home; especially his Mother. He felt excitement within when he thought about telling his family of the adventures he had on this journey. The Sun was not all the way up and it cast a beautiful range of orange and yellow colors across the landscape. Kele joined the others at the fire pit to eat breakfast.

Katori was talking of the last part of the journey, and the importance of everyone being very alert to the perils they still may face. He said, "We all heard the wolves and the panthers last night. The smell of the deer now is getting stronger, and they may stop at nothing to attack us."

Kwahu replied, "We must stay close together as we travel today, and remember to keep our atlatl's and spears close at hand."

Uncle Akando added, "Speaking of that, it would be good if we check all of our things right now to insure we have not dropped anything along the way, and to insure that everything is in good shape."

Everyone, nodding in agreement, went to their baskets to check everything out.

Kele said, "I only have two spear shafts left, and my sandals are getting worn." All the others also had only two or three spear shafts left, and also noted that there sandals were also getting very worn.

Kwahu said, "As we will not be doing any more hunting, there should be enough spear shafts for protection."

They all went about repairing their sandals the best they could, and began gathering up all of their equipment. Katori, Akando, and Kwahu hoisted the deer onto their shoulders; and staying close together in a line, the group began their journey home.

As Kele left the shelter with the group he sensed that there were seemingly hundreds of eyes on them. He knew that the wolves and possibly a Panther were lurking just beyond sight of the small band of humans. He and Attu were bringing up the rear of the line and he knew that if the animals attacked them they would probably come from behind. Keeping a frequent look behind, he thought to himself, "what if they attack us? Will we have enough spears to defend ourselves? Will I be able to move like the wind to avoid their teeth? Will we be able to keep our deer? "

These and many more thoughts raced through his head. He shook his head to clear out the bad thoughts, and turning them into good thoughts. He thought of his being a brave warrior and how his uncles and cousins and he had fought off the Javelina and slain the deer. "I am a brave warrior!" I will paint my story upon the shelter wall when we get home so others may know my adventure, and I will not be defeated no matter what!" he further proclaimed. With these thoughts in his head he began to feel much better as he continued to follow his father and the others on the path.

It seemed like hours to Kele that they had been walking. Kwahu, who was at the head of their small band, turned to the others and said in a quieted voice, "Look up ahead, there are the large rocks above our canyon." Kele and the others were very happy to be nearing the area of their home, and had to restrain themselves from shouting their glee out loud.

Kele and the others came upon the large Boulders and rocks. Kele could hear the wolves now coming closer to the group. Kwahu said "we must get to the boulders quickly, as I sense the wolves may be attacking us soon." All of them agreed that the wolves were coming, and they must seek shelter among the large boulders.

It was'nt long after Kwahu's statement that the wolves began to appear among the brush, and begin their attack. Everyone made a dash into the boulders on the right hand side of the path. Kele, who was taking up the rear of the group, made a very quick decision to head for the Boulders on the left hand side of the trail. Just as the group reached into the boulders the wolves began to attack. Kele squeezed into a crevice between the boulders. He could barely see out, but noticed that the wolves had attacked the others and there was a fight going on. The wolves tried to attack the others from behind, but the boulders were just too large and the wolves just slipped down when they tried to jump up onto the boulders. As boulders were too large for the wolves to attack from above the group, they were doing their best to get into the crevices where the others were. Along with hearing a lot of noise, Kele saw spears jabbing at the wolves, and could tell from the yelps of the wolves when one was stricken.

As everyone was preoccupied with the wolves, Kele did not notice a large panther sneaking up to his position. Suddenly he heard a panting sound, and soft growling sounds. He looked up and he saw the head of the panther looking down upon him. The panther realized that he could not get into the crevice where Kele was but attempted to reach him with his paws. Kele, upon remembering his battle with the javelina, and how he had jabbed him in the mouth with his spear, jabbed at the mouth of the panther. The panther leaped back in pain and tumbled from the boulder. From his hiding place, Kele could see the panther then retreating into the brush, shaking his head and putting his paw to his mouth.

Meanwhile, in the other boulders, the others were still fighting the wolves. Kwahu told the others that "this fight can go on a long time." "We must do something else."

He then told the others to cut off one of the deer's legs, toss it as far away from the boulders that they can, to draw the wolves away from them so they could escape down the path into the canyon.

Kwahu called over to Kele "Kele! Are you all right?

If you are and can hear me, we are going to get the wolves away from us by throwing a leg of deer out. As soon as you see the leg and the wolves run after it, make a fast dash to the canyon trail."

Kele said in the loudest voice that he could muster, "Yes father, I am okay, and I hear you."

Kele watched eagerly for the deer leg to be tossed from his father's position. He then saw the deer leg being tossed high into the air away from the boulders, and the wolves quickly following. Upon seeing this, he grabbed his atlatl and spears and mad a quick dash for the trail. Almost immediately he was joined by the others, leaping, sliding, and tripping down the trail to the bottom of the canyon. Kele kept running down and down, and he could see the river at the bottom of the trail.

Finally reaching the bottom of the trail, the group looked around and above. Kwahu said, "I do not believe the wolves noticed us leaving the big rocks and coming down the trail, I think we are safe from them."

The others agreed. Too exhausted to talk, they all laid down on the ground beside the river and gave great sighs of relief. Attu, Moki, and Kele went to the rivers edge to drink. They splashed, and washed the dirt from their bodies. They were soon accompanied by the uncles, who also drank their fill from the cool water and washed off their dirt.

They were all very tired, especially Kwahu, Katori, and Akando as they were carrying the deer and rabbits down the trail. They all had scratches and sores on their feet, and Katori had a large scratch from a wolf on his right fore-arm. Akando was without a sandal as he had broken a strap on the way down the steep trail. He did not even notice it until now, and showing the others he began to laugh. They all began to laugh at the way he looked. They then began to talk about their battle with wolves and about Kele's fight with the panther.

As Kele and Moki joined in the laughter and the stories with the others, Moki said to Kele, "Where is your necklace?"

Kele looked down and exclaimed with surprise, "My necklace is gone! I must go back to find it."

His father said, "No Kele, we are not going up there. We are not going to take a chance with the panther and the wolves. Besides, you probably lost it during your fight with the panther in the big rocks, and would have trouble finding it. "

Kele was saddened and responded, "I am so sorry father, it took you time to make it and it was so very important to us all."

"It is okay Kele," his father replied, "All of us here know what you did, and losing the necklace does not make you less of a warrior or a man, and there will be more talisman and necklaces for you."

After resting and being quite hungry, the group picked up their game and continued up the path by the river to their shelter home. It was not long until they could see the smoke of the shelter, and some family members down by the river.

Kele was beginning to be relieved that they were finally getting back home. As they finally reached the bottom leading up to the shelter, family members came hopping down to welcome them home. The women took the deer and rabbits from the men and started back up to the shelter, and everyone else followed. Once inside the shelter they all went to the fire pit and began eating.

Once the hunger had subsided they began to tell of their adventure on this hunting journey. Kele was raised into the air by the others and everyone was jubilant on his becoming a man due to his exploits with the deer, javelina, and the panther. He was carried over to the picture wall and he began to paint his story in vibrant yellow and red colors....painting the deer, panther and javelina; his cousins and uncles and himself with spears drawn on atlatl's, and the scenery they encountered. That night, after laying himself down on his sleeping mat and before drifting off to sleep, Kele thought, I am now a warrior, a man, and I am at home with my family. "I had an amazing journey and I am at peace."

EPILOGUE

Eddie and Randy were really looking forward to their vacation at their Grand-Parents ranch near the Big-Bend of West Texas. Summer vacation was finally here, and the 2012 school year was at and end.

After greeting their Grand-Parents, They helped their father unload their ATV 4-wheelers from the trailer, and asked their father if they could take them out on the range for a while.

Their Father said, "You can go riding, but not for long. We have more un-packing to do and then we have to eat supper." He said further, "Do not go too close to that cliff either. I know that you can't drive the 4'wheelers too close because of the large rocks, but I do not want you walking too close to the edge either."

They listened and told their Father they would not take too long and they would be careful. They were so eager to ride their 4-wheelers.

They rode for a while, and went over by the rocks at the rim of the great cliff. "Remember when Grand-pa and Dad took us down into the canyon to that Rock Shelter in the cliff?" said Eddie.

Randy replied, "Yes, and we found that neat arrow-head inside. It is a big shelter. There must have been a lot of people using it over the thousands of years."

They then turned their 4 wheelers to go to the house, when Randy saw something shining from inside the large boulders. Stopping his engine, he got off of the ATV and went over to the Rocks. He stooped down and picked it up. "Look," he said to Eddie, "it's a necklace. It has colored stones on it and in the middle is a large tooth."

"That's a javelina tusk Randy," said Eddie. "And the necklace still has some sort of old cord holding it together. " It is some kind of old Indian necklace. Let's hurry and get to the house so we can show Dad and Grandpa." Saying that, they started their 4-wheelers and headed to the house, admiring their find on the way.

CPSIA information can be obtained
at www.ICGtesting.com
Printed in the USA
LVIW010409230412
278425LV00001B